He's her brother's best friend.
She's his best friend's little sister.
What could possibly go wrong?

Published by DL Gallie Author (c)

First published in the Summer Heat Anthology 18 May 2020

Second release 11th January 2021

Cover designed by **Tash Drake**, Outlined with Love Design

Edited by **Karen Hrdlicka**, Barren Acres Editing

Proofread by **Lana Clark**

Formatting and interior design by **DL Gallie**

I've had a crush on Lawson O'Connor since forever but it can never be, he's my older brother's best friend.

I always thought the feelings were one-sided but recently, I'm beginning to suspect otherwise.

A subtle touch here.
An inappropriate comment there.
A smoldering look.
A sexy wink.

And then it happens, we hook up.

It's everything I ever imagined and more but we can never be, can we?

ALSO BY DL GALLIE

STAND ALONES

Out of Nowhere

Antecedent

Seven Nights

Doc Steel

Oops

Summer Heat

In the Dark of Night anthology

FALLING NOVELS

Falling for Dr. Kelly

Falling for Dr. Knight

Falling for Agent Cox

Falling for Agent Cruz - coming early 2021

THE UNEXPECTED SERIES

When it comes to love, expect the unexpected

The Unexpected Gift

The Unexpected Letter

The Unexpected Package

The Unexpected Connection

THE CASTAWAY GROVE COLLECTION

Love has arrived in the Grove

Oasis

Unequivocal Love

Five Words

Broken Rules

...and a few more as well.

THE LIQUOR CABINET SERIES

Liquor has never been so disturbingly saucy

Malt Me (Book 1)

Tequila Healing (Book 2)

Wine Not (Book 3)

The Final Shot (Book 4)

The Liquor Cabinet: Series boxset

The course of true love never did run smooth.

~ *William Shakespeare*

Prologue

Always the bridesmaid, never the bride.

That's the running joke in our group of friends. Seems all my besties are getting hitched. Hell, even my brother is about to get married. Then there's me, the single one. I'm pretty good at finding Mr. Not-So-Right or Mr. Douche, I have that down to a fine T, but finding Mr. Right, that's been a little harder. But when I compare everyone to *him,* it's tough for anyone live up to the pedestal I've put my dream man on.

Lawson O'Connor has been my secret—not so secret —crush since I was a little girl. I've been in love with him for as long as I can remember. He also happens to be my big brother, Travis' best friend, therefore he's relegated in the 'never gonna happen' category. There's the unwritten Bro Code rule that you never date your best friend's little sister. Plus there's the little fact Travis would probably kill us both; damn you, Travis Nathaniel Templeton—yes

I middle named him, that's how hot Lawson is—and your choice of best friends. Lawson and Trav have been best friends since middle school and the first time ten-year-old me laid eyes on my brother's best friend, I thought he was the most beautiful boy ever. Move over Leo DiCaprio—my then crush—there's a new hottie in town.

What started out as an innocent schoolgirl crush when I was ten, turned into an infatuation the older, and hotter, Lawson got. He grew into a six foot tall, perfectly sculptured man. Dark chocolate brown hair. Tanned skin. Blue eyes that bore into your soul, and turn you into a wanton, panting mess. Ohh and I can't forget his dimples, yes dimples. Those lil' indents in his cheeks make me weak at the knees. And the icing on the Lawson O'Connor cake, his voice—sigh. He has the voice of a god, it's deep, husky, and it does things to me that are kinda awkward when my brother and parents are around.

In my dreams, I dream Lawson and I are blissfully in love, but that will never ever happen...or so I thought.

Chapter One

LAWSON

STANDING AT THE FRONT OF THE CHAPEL, I'M sweating my ass off in my monkey suit, as I stand here waiting for the ceremony to get underway, where childhood sweethearts Tayla and Corbin get married. The wedding music starts, the doors to the chapel open, and in walks the first bridesmaid and my jaw hits the floor when my gaze lands on Mia Templeton. Even though she's wearing a hideous—once again—bridesmaid dress, she looks sexy as fuck. *When did she become such a babe?* My eyes roam over her as she walks down the aisle, a smile graces her face. She has never looked so stunning. My cock twitches and I swallow deeply. As I continue to stare at her, it hits me that she's not Travis' little sister anymore, now she's Travis' smokin' fuckin' hot little sister. *Oh shit, I'm in trouble.*

When I realize I'm checking out Trav's little sis, I mentally slap myself. Everyone knows the best friend's sister, littler or big, is off-limits. It's an unwritten rule from the dawn of time, but fuck me, when did Mia become so hot?

I'm screwed, and not in the 'wham-bam-thank-you-ma'am' kind of way. I'm screwed in the 'she's-off-limits-you-touch-her-you-die' kind of way.

Closing my eyes and taking a deep breath, I start thinking about fat saggy granny boobs. I can't be sporting a boner right now because A. I'm standing in a chapel where my friends are about to get married and B. The chick in question is off-limits since she's related to my best friend and C. I don't feel like being murdered today.

From next to me Trav tries to cover a laugh but fails miserably, the glare he receives from Andrea, the matron of honor, instantly has me standing up straight and my cock hanging his head back down; good boy. I knew he was my best friend for a reason. *Thank you for laughing and garnering a murderous look*, I think to myself as Tayla reaches the altar and takes Corbin's hands. They look sickly in love, it kinda makes me want to vomit, but if any two people are meant to be together, it's these two.

The ceremony gets underway but my eyes keep drifting over to Mia. She catches me looking at her and the sneaky devil sticks her tongue out at me, I bite the inside of my cheek to hold back my laugh. That's such a Mia thing to do. I've known her since I met Trav in middle school. She's always just been Trav's little sister, but right now, she's a bridesmaid I want to hook up with, and I don't know what to do about that. This is uncharted territory but if I want to continue breathing, I need to put how fucking sexy she looks out of my mind and focus on the nuptials of our friends. If Trav gets wind of the dirty thoughts I currently have about Mia, I'd be strung up by my balls before the happy couple get to their I do's.

The ceremony is over and Tayla and Corbin are finally husband and wife. Thankfully, my cock decided to play dead and he has not popped back up to say 'hey congrats' to the happy couple. My eyes are looking everywhere but at Mia, but with us both being in the bridal party, it's hard—pun no intended—to avoid her. It's like since I've noticed her beauty I'm subconsciously seeking her out like a crack whore needing her next fix.

I'm watching her with Mom and Dad Templeton and I find myself smiling. Trav drapes his arm around my shoulder, "Let's get wedding drunk." Usually I'd be all over that but tonight, with these new developments, I need a clear head but I can fake it...right?

Chapter Two

MIA

...two weekends later

"I SEE WE MEET AGAIN," A VOICE SAYS FROM MY SIDE. Turning my head, I look to where the sound came from and smile. My panties also dampen, but that's nothing new when it comes to *him*.

"I'm starting to think you're stalking me," I tease.

"You could have a worse guy as a stalker," he boldy replies with a wink. "He definitely wouldn't be as good looking or as charismatic as I am."

Ovaries boom.

"Someone's got a big ego."

He shrugs in that sexy nonchalant way and says, "It's not the only thing that's big."

My eyes bug open and then my gaze drops to his crotch. Lifting it back up to his face, he winks at me and we continue staring at one another for a few beats. Right at this moment, I wish I could lean over, grip his cheeks in my palms, and press my lips to his. Slip my tongue inside his mouth. Run my hands over his sexy as sin body. Fu...the sound of his voice snaps me back to reality.

"Huh?"

"Mia, I asked, how you are?"

"I'm a bridesmaid...again."

"Well, I can unequivocally say, you are the sexiest bridesmaid here...like usual."

"Someone needs to lay off the beers and get their eyes checked."

"My eyesight is just fine, spank you very much. And this is beer number two. I'm just stating the obvious, Mia. You are sexy as hell in that lemon yellow tulle inspired number, which I so happen to think would look much better on the floor."

Holy fuck, Lawson O'Connor is flirting with me...I think.

Have I had one too many cocktails?

This cannot be happening, any minute now I'm going to wake up. Or I'll see he's flirting with the person beside me.

I look to my left and no one is there.

I look to the right and again, no one is there.

It's just Lawson and me.

Looking up, I see him staring intently at me. He wolfishly smiles and it hits me, holy fuck, Lawson Templeton *is* flirting with me.

What.

The.

Actual.

Fuck!

"Would you like to dance?" he asks.

Words elude me right now as I process what's happening. Well, what I *think* is happening. Lawson is flirting with me and asking me to dance. Have I crossed into the *Twilight Zone*, because this cannot be real?

My eyes drop to his outstretched hand then back up to his face. He lowers his hand, rejection written on his face, but also concern. I'm unable to speak and reassure him that I'm not a complete moron, but for the first time in my life, I have nothing to say.

"Mia?" he probes again, the deep timbre of his voice reverberates through my body. "Are you okay?" I manage to nod my head, and that motion eases his worry and once again, he smiles.

Ovaries BOOM; again.

"Do you want to dance?"

Still I cannot find my voice so I silently nod my head up and down. He smiles again but this time it's like he's hit the jackpot, when in reality, he's just dancing with me. My eyes are locked on him, he winks at me and I swear, it shoots right between my thighs. My clit furiously pulsating from the intensity of his gaze. I'm in shock and totally turned on. My body is sparking to life and I'm tempted to say, "Fuck it" and throw myself at him. My cheeks are heating and I swallow deeply to calm my nerves. I'm pretty sure he knows what's currently happening between my thighs, because he just eye-fucked the hell out of me.

He plucks my drink from my hand, places it on the table, takes my hand in his, and escorts me onto the dance floor. We reach the center and he spins me to face him. He slides his hand around my waist, pulling me close to his body. So close I can feel the hard planes of his chest against my body. My arms lift on their own accord and I drape them over his shoulders. His other hand sits low on my back. Our bodies sway to "At Last" by Etta James. Everything around me fades away. It's just us, and Etta. We stare into each other's eyes and something passes between us. Our heads slowly move but the moment is interrupted when my dear old brother growls, "Hands off my sister's ass, O'Connor."

"She wishes my hands were on her ass," he playfully shoots back at my brother, garnering a gaze that would cut stone from Trav.

Yes, yes, I do wish your hands were on my ass, I think to myself, but rather than saying that out loud, I shake my head and glare at my brother. "He wishes his hands were on my ass."

Then my mouth drops open when I hear Lawson quietly mumble, "Hell yes, I do." It's only loud enough for me to hear but that comment definitely confirms it.

Lawson-fucking-O'Connor *IS* flirting with me.

My eyes flick up to his and he winks. My G-string —'cause this hideous bridesmaid dress wouldn't allow for any other style—is now soaked and close to combusting from the heat coursing through my body right now. Before I can process, or enjoy, what's happening with Lawson, I'm pulled from his arms and I'm now dancing with my brother. Trav is chatting away, but I have no clue as to what he is saying or what I reply. My eyes keep darting over to Lawson, who is now dancing with Sydney,

Travis's fiancée, and each time they do, I see him staring back at me. When our gaze meets, he winks or blows a cocky kiss at me.

What the hell is happening right now? Any minute now, I'm going to wake up, alone, in my bed. This must be a dream because there's no way in hell Lawson is flirting with me.

Chapter Three

LAWSON

THANK FUCK TRAV DECIDED TO CUT IN WHEN HE DID, because I was so close to taking Mia's face between my palms and kissing the life out of her. If I had of done that; A. I would have ruined Tayla and Corbin's wedding because Travis would have killed me right here in the middle of the dancefloor and B. Travis would have killed me.

As I twirl around the room with Sydney, I keep trying to think of her as little annoying Mia, but right now, it's fucking impossible. She's sexy as fuck Mia. My eyes keep drifting to her and I'm eye-fucking the hell out of her right now.

"You okay?" Sydney asks me.

Her voice snaps my attention to her. "Yeah, just been a long week."

"Mmmhmpf." She nods but from the look in her eye, she knows I'm full of shit. My suspicion is confirmed when her eyes dart over to Mia. Then she looks back at me and smirks. *Saucy bitch.*

The song comes to an end and I take the opportunity to leave before Syd gets me gossiping like a schoolgirl. I don't know how Syd does it, but she always gets me to open up and this is one secret, or what-ever-the-fuck-this-is, that I will take to my grave because I kinda like my balls where they are and I really like breathing too. If Travis got wind of me crushing on his lil' sis, me and the guys down below are fucked; and not in the naked sweaty fun way.

Exiting the ballroom, I head to the bathroom. After taking a piss, I walk outside to get some air because clearly there's a noxious gas that's making me go fucking nuts for Mia. Yeah that must be it, I'm not really attracted to Mia, I'm just tripping but when I step outside and my eyes land on her, I know I'm not.

I'm attracted to my best friend's little sister...Oops!

Chapter Four

MIA

"Sooo," Travis probes, as soon as he pulls me away from Lawson, "how you doin?"

"As good as can be expected when I look like," I lower my head and take in the monstrosity of a bridesmaid dress I'm currently wearing, "a—"

"Giant fucking lemon!"

Smacking him in the arm, I shake my head. "Yeah, that. I friggin' hope Syd picks us nice dresses. Why do brides always do this? It's like they want us to suffer and for all the attention to be on them." Travis eyes me, "Okay, fair enough, the attention should be on them for their special day and I get they want the focus on them, but it can be done without making those who are helping them look like a lemon...or Little Bo Peep...or a turd?"

Travis laughs, "I still can't believe Lana made you guys wear a dress that color and in that shape."

"It wasn't too bad...until she added the white I-look-like-eyes bow to the waist."

"You guys really looked like poop emojis."

"That is one bridesmaid dress I'm trying to forget but those pics are all over FB and Insta. If I ever get married, I want my bridesmaids to wear a simple spaghetti strapped cocktail dress in deep plum...or I'll just elope and not do the whole wedding thing."

"Really?" Trav questions me, "I thought you'd want the whole princess wedding thing?"

"Do you even know me at all? I'm the least girly girl there is, and I HATE being the center of attention."

"All true. Okay, for shits and giggles, if you were to do the wedding thing, what would your ideal one be?"

Thinking for a moment, I smile when I imagine Lawson and I standing on a beach, gazing into each other's eyes. Holding hands. The sea breeze blowing around us. Waves crashing to the shore.

"Well?" The sound of Travis' voice ends that vision.

"My dream wedding is on a beach. In Bora Bora. It's just me, my husband-to-be, you and Syd, Mom and Dad, and his parents, and siblings, if he has any. Simple yet elegant."

"That's totally you, Mia. Whoever you end up with will be a lucky guy."

"He's a lucky imaginary guy. I'm probably going to end up the crazy cat lady."

"Well you've got the crazy down pat," Trav teases. "But seriously, you'll meet Mr. Right. Hell, you might have already met him and you just don't know it yet." He pauses and then cockily adds, "You can be slow at times."

"Hey," I scoff, but he's right, I'm not the sharpest tool in the shed, and neither is he actually.

Travis and I go quiet and we continue to sway to the music. My eyes drift over to Lawson, and once again I catch him watching me. Well, I think he's watching me.

This is totally tripping me out, I swear he's flirting with me. Lawson-freaking-O'Connor is flirting with me, but am I mistaking this and making it into something more because I've always wanted more when it comes to him? He's always been friendly with me, but it's only ever been in the sister-from-another-mister way.

Clearly I've had too much bubbly because there's no way he is...is there?

Chapter Five

MIA

...three weekends later

Once again I'm in a bridesmaid dress but thankfully this time, I'm not wearing a hideous one. Raine picked us these fabulously stunning, floor-length, strapless A-line gowns with a sweetheart neckline and a pleated bodice in a rich reddish chocolate brown color. On our feet are strappy gold heels that are actually comfortable—thank you, Raine, for picking something beautiful, and comfy.

The ceremony passes by quickly—thank you again, Raine—there's nothing worse than a wedding ceremony that drags on and on and on. The minister declares them husband and wife and says those five magical words, "You may kiss your bride." Jenson grips Raine's cheeks in his palms and their first kiss as man and wife is perfect. I have to look away when it turns heated. My eyes land on

Lawson's in the crowd and he's staring intently at me. He winks and then turns his attention to Sydney. He glances back at me and the look in his eyes has my insides quivering. It's full of hunger and want...for me.

Ever since Tayla and Corbin's wedding the other week, things between us are different. It seems like Lawson is always flirting with me. He's now finding ways to subtly touch me or be close by. He's definitely acting strange, especially when Travis is around, and since we are finalizing everything for his and Syd's wedding, we are all together...a lot.

I'm whisked away for photos and other bridesmaid crap, and finally, we make it to the reception. Taking a seat at the bridal table, I'm handed another glass of champagne. Chugging back the bubbly liquid, I place the empty flute down and close my eyes for a moment. Savoring the crispness of the bubbles on my tongue.

Opening my eyes, I startle when I see Lawson standing in front of me. "Mia," he croons.

"Lawson," I say in reply, as my eyes rake over him. How does he manage to make a dress shirt and slacks look so fucking sexy? The top few buttons are undone, he's since rolled the sleeves up to his elbows, showing off his muscly forearms. Finally my gaze makes its way up to his face and I notice he's staring intently at me.

"You are a vision," he says, before someone yells his name. He winks, turns around ,and walks away from me.

My mouth drops open as his words register in my mind.

"You okay, Mia?" Tayla asks, as she slides into the chair next to me.

Nodding my head, I turn my attention from a retreating Lawson and focus on Tayla. "Yeah, I think I drank that glass of bubbly too quickly." I focus on the empty glass but my gaze wanders back to Lawson, who is chatting with Sydney, Travis, and a few other friends.

"Mmmhmpf," she replies. "Or does it have something to do a certain guy who has been eye-fucking you all day?"

My head snaps toward her. "What?"

"Don't play coy with me. You've had a crush on Lawson since forever and I think he has one on you too. I noticed how you two were acting at my wedding."

"Pffft, you need to lay off the bubbly."

"Hell no," she scoffs, we both laugh. "I'm just calling it as I see it." She rests her hand on my forearm. "Mia, if two people are meant to be, it's you guys."

"But what about Travis?"

"What about him?" She flags down a waiter and grabs two more glasses of champagne. She hands one to me and takes a sip of hers.

"They are best friends. Isn't there an unwritten rule about sisters being off-limits? She's like forbidden fruit."

"Since when have you followed the rules?" I roll my eyes at her but she's right, I never follow the rules. I'm the ultimate rule breaker. "Mia, just go for it."

"What if I fuck up their friendship? I couldn't live with myself if that happened."

"But what if it doesn't? Just think about it."

With that she stands up and makes her way over to Corbin. When he sees her, he stands up, takes the glass from her hand, places it on the table next to him, and just like at their wedding, he grips her cheeks and kisses her. Everyone around them hoots and hollers but they don't care, they are blissfully in love with one another and I want that. I really want that...with Lawson.

My gaze drifts back to him and once again, he's staring at me. Bringing my glass to my lips, I take a sip and decide to go for it...what's the worst that could happen?

Chapter Six

LAWSON

Fuck me sideways, Mia is stunning today.

When she stepped into the chapel, my jaw hit the floor. Actually, when I think about it, over the last few weeks since Corbin and Tayla's wedding, I've noticed *everything* about her. The cute dimple on her chin. The sway of her hips when she walks. Her infectious laugh. How the blue of her eyes pops when she's excited. The tinge of pink that covers her cheeks when she's embarrassed. The plumpness of her lips...and how they'd look wrapped around my dick. Shaking my head, I quickly get rid of those thoughts, because her brother is sitting right next to me and I'm in a house of God where my friends are about to get hitched.

The ceremony passes by in a blur and we are now at the reception, awaiting the arrival of the wedding party. My mind drifts back to the ceremony, throughout the whole thing, my eyes were glued to Mia. Thankfully it looked like I was just watching the proceedings, but in reality, I was eye-fucking the one woman I should never be eye-fucking. I was imagining myself stripping her out of that sexy as fuck bridesmaid dress and all the deliciously wicked things I want to do to her body.

Readjusting myself, I turn my gaze to the conversation happening between Corbin and Travis but my mind, well it's still in dirty town with Mia.

"What the fuck is up with you?" Travis says, snapping my attention to him.

"Huh?" I reply like a chump.

"You're off your game today."

"Am not," I scoff in reply.

"Are too."

"Am not."

"Are—"

"Oh my God," Sydney interrupts, "you two are acting like children." She snaps, as she hands out beers to the guys while Reese places two wine glasses on the table and proceeds to fill them for her and Sydney.

"Am not," we both say in unison.

Everyone laughs, everyone but Sydney that is. She shakes her head and sighs. Taking her wine from Reese. Her gaze—which is on fire by the way—flicks between the two of us. "Grow up, you morons, we are at a wedding for fuck's sake," she snarls, clearly not impressed with our goofing around.

And again, in unison, we singsong, "Yes, Mom."

This garners a smirk from her and just like that we are off the hook; phew. The conversation turns to the

NHL—go Kings—and Travis and I fall back into our usual banter, and I forget about sexy times with Mia.

It's all going well until the wedding party arrives and like a heat-seeking missile, my eyes lock on to Mia. Her cheeks are flushed, a sure sign she's had a few wines. Her head is thrown back and she's laughing at something her partner says, and then I notice him holding her hand and I become ragey. Internally growling *Mine*.

"She looks beautiful," Sydney says.

"Yeah, Mia is stunning today," I reply, her head snaps to me. "What?"

"I was referring to the bride."

"Ohh," I say, as Sydney stares at me, her eyes full of questions. Before she can ask, the emcee announces that dinner will be served shortly and we are to make our way to our assigned table. Like a herd of cattle, we make our way into the dining area. We find our table in the far back corner—aptly dubbed the naughty corner—and sit down. Corbin is to my left, he's solo tonight since Tayla is also a bridesmaid. To my right is Sydney, and from the glances she keeps giving me, I know that sometime this evening I will be having a conversation with her...about Mia. That girl misses nothing and my slip of the tongue earlier, just added fuel to the fire. Oops.

Chapter Seven

MIA

THE SPEECHES ARE OVER AND MY STOMACH IS SORE, Jensen's best man gave THE best wedding speech ever. He had everyone laughing but at the same time it was heartfelt and beautiful. You can tell that he and Jensen have a tight friendship and bond; much like Lawson and Travis. I know earlier I decided to go for it with Lawson, but what if it ruins their friendship? I can't be held responsible for that, maybe it's best if I just leave it be.

GAH, I don't know.

I'm so lost in my own head that I don't realize he's standing in front of me until he clears his throat. Lifting my head, I gaze into his eyes and with that one look something passes between us. Something has definitely changed, and I think tonight will be the night we either sink or swim; move over Rose, there's room for both of us on that door...I hope.

"May I have this dance?" The deep timbre of his

voice ripples through my body, lighting my insides up like fireworks on the Fourth.

He offers me his hand. My eyes drop to it, then back to his face. Words elude me right now, I've never been like this before around Lawson but right now, I'm mute. Finally, my brain clicks into gear and with a smile, I nod. "I'd love to." Placing my palm in his, an electrical current zaps up my arm, causing my breath to hitch. From the look on Lawson's face, he felt it too.

Inhaling deeply, I follow Lawson onto the dance floor. My heart is racing right now and my panties are damp with arousal. He spins me around and pulls me into him. My breasts pressing into his hard chest, he slides his hand around my waist. My skin tingling under his touch. Lifting my gaze to his, and he winks. My lips lift in a smile when he spins me out and pulls me back in before dipping me backward. A squeal breaks free and when he pulls me upright again, I giggle like a schoolgirl.

Sliding my arms around his neck, I rest my head on his chest and we sway to the music, the melody enveloping us. Everything disappears. It's just the two of us, under the twinkling lights of the dance floor.

I don't know how many songs pass but Lawson and I stay on the dance floor, wrapped in each other's embrace. It isn't until the lights flicker on that we realize the evening has come to an end. We stop dancing and stare at one another. The air around us crackling, I've never felt like this with him before.

Before I can register what's happening, Lawson takes my hand in his and drags me out of the reception room and toward the elevators. He punches the call button and as if the gods are on our side, the doors immediately open. He steps into the waiting car and pulls me in behind him. Pressing the button for the seventh floor, the doors close. Lawson turns to face me. We stare at one another and the temperature in the elevator becomes stifling. My tongue darts out and I bite on my bottom lip. A guttural growl comes from Lawson. His eyes are locked on my lips, his breathing hurried.

The elevator doors open and again without saying a word, he takes my hand in his and pulls me toward his room. He stops and removes the room key out of his pocket, he looks at me and without saying anything, I know this is it: this is the moment Lawson-fucking-O'Connor is going to kiss me. My breathing picks up, my chest rapidly rising with each breath. He takes a step toward me, he lowers his head down; I can feel his breath on my lips. I wait for that first contact but the kiss never comes.

Opening my eyes, I see he's frozen. His eyes are locked on mine. I know he wants it so I decide to take control. Lifting my hands, I grip his cheeks and I kiss him. I close my eyes and press my lips to his. Time stands still, our lips are pressed together and neither of us moves. Fear seeps in but then, I feel his tongue move against my lips. Opening my mouth, I invite him in. And he doesn't disappoint, he slips his tongue inside and begins fucking my mouth. Sliding my hands around his neck, I pull him into me, deepening our kiss. As first kisses go, this is the best one ever in the history of kisses.

The ding of the elevator separates us, when the doors open; we hear Trav's voice. My eyes bulge out of my head and my heart starts racing, and not in the fun sexy way that it just was. Ohh fuck, all my fears are about to come true. Trav is gonna kill Lawson in the hotel hallway. Then quicker than Speedy Gonzales, Lawson unlocks the door, grabs my hand, and pulls me into his room for a night that will change everything.

Chapter Eight

LAWSON

Holy fuck that was close.

Holy fuck, Mia Templeton and I just kissed. Well, she kissed me but after a micro second, I kissed her back.

It was perfect.

It was amazing.

Holy shit, I kissed Mia Templeton.

It was everything a first kiss should be...and then her brother, my best friend, almost caught us. *Fuuuuck!*

It's dark inside my hotel room, the only sound is our heavy breathing and the thudding of our hearts. For a brief moment, I'm unsure of what to do next but just like over the last few weeks, I'm drawn to Mia by an invisible force. Something compels me and I gently push Mia against the wall and cover her mouth with mine. Our tongues slide together. Our hands roam each other's bodies.

The kiss outside was soft and sensual, this kiss is carnal and full of hunger.

She drapes her arms over my shoulders and pulls me toward her. She's kissing me back with just as much vigor. My hands cup her cheeks and I let the kiss and Mia consume me. Our tongues slip in and out of each other's mouth. "Lawson," she murmurs against my lips, that one word causes me to lose control. Sliding my hands down her body, I grip the hem of her dress and lift it over her head. Our lips briefly separate as the silky material passes but as soon as we can, we once again devour each other's mouth.

Dropping her dress to the carpet, I place my hands under to taut perfect ass and lift her up. She wraps her legs around my waist. I can feel the heat of her pussy against my skin. I groan into the kiss as I turn around and walk into the room. Heading for the bed, I gently lower her to the mattress. The curtains are open, the moonlight illuminating Mia's beauty. "Fuck me, Mia, you are gorgeous." Her face breaks out in a smile, her tongue darts out, and she licks her bottom lip.

"Please, Lawson," she pleads.

Lifting my hands, I untuck my shirt and begin unbuttoning it. Mia sits up and shimmies toward me at the end of the bed. She pushes my hands out of the way and with her eyes on mine, she finishes undoing the buttons. Sliding her hands across my shoulder blades, she pushes the material of my shirt down my arms. I'm left standing in my dress pants but not for long. Kicking off my shoes, she makes quick work of my belt, button, and fly. She slides her hand around my waist and tugs down my briefs and pants. Kicking them off, I stand before her naked as the day I was born. Her eyes roam over my body and she licks her lip again. Gripping her cheeks in my palms, I lower my head and press my lips to her again.

Stepping back I gaze at her. She pulls away from me and sits back, she lifts her foot up, and goes to undo the strap on her shoes. "No," I roughly say, pressing my hand over hers. "I want to fuck you with them on."

Mia nods and lies back on the bed, she beckons me forward with her finger and like a moth to a flame, I climb onto the mattress and crawl up her. Gently blowing on her skin as I go, her body erupts in goosebumps...but she won't be cold for long. Cocooning her under me, I stare down at her. Her blonde hair fans out underneath her like a halo, lowering my head I kiss her. It starts out soft but quickly turns hungry. My cock is harder than a rock and I cannot wait to sink myself inside her.

Mia reaches behind her and unclasps her bra. Slipping the straps down her arms, I throw the item to the floor and lower my head to her breast. My tongue circles her nipple before I take the stiff peak into my mouth, sucking and biting her flesh. "Lawson," she moans, as she runs her fingernails over my scalp. Kissing down her stomach, she writhes in pleasure beneath me. Reaching her panties, I kiss her mound through the silky material. Sucking her clit through the material, I rub her lips with my finger. The material is soaked, and not from my mouth. Pushing the material to the side, I slide my finger between her folds. She's drenched and I cannot wait to fuck her but first, I want her to let loose against my fingers and mouth. "Mia, I'm not going to fuck you until you soak my fingers and face."

"Lawson," she groans, as she grips my head and shoves it into her farther. Her panties are in the way and I don't want to wait, I grip the material on either side of her hips and tear them from her body, dropping the shredded material to the floor. Baring her smooth pussy to me. With a grin, I lower my head down and feast on her. Licking and sucking her folds, she tastes amazing. Slipping a finger into her, I focus on her clit, sucking and nipping as I pump my fingers in and out of her. "Lawson," she mewls as her body stiffens and she explodes. Her juices coating my face and fingers as she reaches her peak.

Lifting my head, I stare up at her. She's glowing from her orgasm and I can't wait to fuck her.

Chapter Nine

MIA

Holy shit, that was an intense orgasm. It was *the* most intense amazing orgasm of my life. Opening my eyes, I see Lawson staring at me, I can't believe said orgasm was from him. Never in my wildest dreams did I ever think this would happen...and reality, is so much better than my dreams. The look in his eyes is carnal and heated. Even though I just came, I'm ready for more. After one time I'm hooked. I could quite easily become an addict because Lawson O'Connor is a fucking god with his tongue and fingers. I can only imagine what he can do with his dick.

I'm normally shy and reserved in bed, but Lawson brings out my inner minx and she's ready to play again. Lifting my finger, I beckon him to me, widening my legs at the same time so he knows exactly what I want. To my shock, he climbs off the bed, I start to panic and think he regrets it. He must sense the change in me because he shakes his head, "I'm just grabbing a condom, Mia. There's no way in hell I'm not fucking you tonight." *Thank fuck for that.*

I watch him as he picks up his pants, grabs his wallet, and pulls out a foil packet. Ripping it open with his teeth, he quickly sheaths his cock. My eyes are locked on his dick. Dicks aren't the most attractive looking appendage but I shit you not, Lawson's is the most beautiful cock I've ever seen in my life. I cannot wait to feel it inside of me. If this is all a dream and I wake up alone in the morning, I think I'll be okay because this is the best dream in the history of dreams.

My mind flits back to the present when Lawson lifts my leg and kisses my ankle. His lips skim up my calf, along my thigh, he skips between my legs and continues to kiss up my stomach, between my breasts, up my neck, along my jawline, and finally my lips. His tongue licks along my seam and slips inside. While down below, he teases me with his dick. Pressing it against my lower lips and pulling back, repeating this over and over.

Griping his cheeks, I stare into his eyes, they are bluer than I've ever seen them. "Lawson, just fuck me."

We stare at one another intently. He winks and then hall-a-fucking-luljah he finally enters me. For a brief second it hurts but the pain is quickly replaced with pleasure as he thrusts in and out of me, hitting that magic spot each time. Our eyes are fused on one another as he picks up his pace. His hips pistoning back and forth. In and out.

Lifting my legs, I dig the heel of my shoes into his ass, garnering a hiss from him. With a smirk I throw my arms over his shoulders and pull him down to kiss me. He kisses me with an intensity I've never felt before. My body is tingling, I never want this to end but at the same time I do, I need to come.

"Let go, Mia," he croons again my lips.

His words set me off and I crash over the edge. My body zinging as pleasure courses through me from head to toe. Above me, I feel Lawson tense and on the next thrust, he too comes. Grunting though his release, he pistons his hips violently, causing me to explode again. "Laaaawsssoooon," I moan, as orgasm number three ripples through me.

Lawson pulls out and collapses onto the mattress next to me. We both lie here heavily panting. A few moments later, he hops up and walks into the bathroom, and when he returns, he has a warm wet washcloth. He cleans between my thighs and then returns the cloth to the bathroom.

Before climbing back into bed, he removes my shoes. When he lies down, he pulls me into his side and places a gentle kiss on my temple. This gesture causes my body to break out in goosebumps and I shiver. He mistakes it as me being cold, he reaches down and pulls the sheet up. He moves me closer to him. "Night, Mia," he whispers.

"Night, Lawson," I reply.

He drifts off to sleep immediately but I lie in his arms, wide awake. Eventually I drift off to sleep, wrapped in Lawson's arms with a smile on my face.

Best. Wedding. Ever!

The sun shining into my eyes causes me to wake up and I'm disoriented for a few moments, and the dream I had last night comes crashing back to me. With a smile on my face, I turn my head and my eyes bug wide open when I realize, it wasn't a dream. I am indeed naked and in bed with Lawson. My body aches in the most delicious way, and it hits me that I had the best night of my life last night with the man of my dreams.

Rolling to my back, I stare at the ceiling and hope I can feel like this again. I pray with everything I have that this wasn't just a drunken wedding hookup, but Lawson is Trav's best friend, it can never be more...can it?

Chapter Ten

LAWSON

Waking the next morning, I'm pleasantly surprised to find Mia still here. And what's even more amazing, she's still snuggled into my side, just like we were last night after the best fucking sex of my life...with Mia...Trav's baby sister. I was positive she'd have snuck out during the night. I was so sure that I would have bet my left nut on me being alone this morning. Definitely glad I didn't take that bet, I like the boys just where they are...that is if Trav doesn't find out. He would kill me for sure and that puts me in a fucked-up situation. I may lose my best friend but I may also lose Mia, and I don't want to lose either of them. Fuuuuck, this is so shitty.

Mia nuzzles into my side, bringing my thoughts away from all the possible shitty scenarios, but when I look down and see her staring at me with the most gorgeous smile on her face, all those doubts disappear. "Morning,"

I offer, lowering my head down for a kiss. She turns her head and nuzzles into my chest shaking her head.

"No kisses. I have morning breath."

"And?"

"Umm it's eeeew."

"Mia, I had my mouth on your pussy last night, pretty sure I can handle morning breath, now lift your head and let me kiss you good morning."

She lifts her head and rolls half on top of me, leaning down and before I can kiss her, she slides over me, climbs off, and heads into the bathroom. If she thinks that's going to stop me, she's sorely mistaken. Climbing out, I step into the bathroom, reach out, grab her hand, spin her toward me, and before she can protest, I cover her mouth with mine. She's frozen for a few moments and I start to think I've overstepped the mark, but after what feels like an eternity, she grips my cheeks in her palms and kisses me back.

I fucking love kissing Mia Templeton.

Breaking the kiss I stare at her. Her lips are plump and swollen. Her cheeks are tinged pink and her eyes are ablaze with lust and hunger. She turns to the sink, grabs my toothbrush, and begins to brush her teeth.

"So, you wouldn't kiss me due to morning breath, but you're happy to share my toothbrush?" I question, leaning against the vanity to watch her brush her teeth...with MY toothbrush.

She shrugs her shoulders and continues to brush her teeth. When she's finished, she spits, rinses the sink and my brush, and then applies more toothpaste. "Here," she says, offering me the toothbrush. Taking the brush from her, I brush my teeth with my gaze locked on her.

When I'm finished I spit, rinse, and step to the shower, flicking the water on, I turn to face Mia. "Shower?"

She nods, walks around me, and climbs in. I step in behind her and watch as she moves under the spray. She drops her head back and lets the water cascade down her sexy as fuck body. I've seen Mia in swimsuits since we were kids, but I've never noticed her body before, but fuck me, she is the epitome of a sex siren. She turns to face me and just like last night, a force takes over my body. I step toward her and press her gently into the tile wall and slam my lips to hers. I fuck her mouth with my tongue, devouring her as if she's my last meal.

"Mia," I murmur against her lips. "I need you."

"You have me," she replies as she presses on my chest, pushing me back. She drops to her knees and before I can register what's about to happen, she takes my dick into her mouth and sucks, the head hitting the back of her throat.

"Fuuuuck!" I moan.

"After this," she says before sucking my cock back into her mouth. Mia continues suck my cock and fondles my balls, sooner than I'd like to admit, I come down her throat. Surprising me, she swallows every last drop. Rising up, she stares at me and raises her eyebrows seductively.

Dropping to my knees, I lift her leg over my shoulder, flatten my tongue, and lick her from taint to clit.

"Fuuuuck!" she mewls.

Cockily, I look up at her. "After this." Before she can reply, I press my face back to her pussy and I lick, suck, and finger her to her first orgasm of the day.

Pushing to my feet, I raise my eyebrows at her and it's game on. We step to one another and it's a free-for-all. Hands roam each other's bodies. Our teeth bump in our frenzied kisses. Placing my hands under her ass, just like last night she wraps her legs around my waist and I press her into the tiles before slamming my dick into her.

We fuck.

It's hard.

It's fast.

It's carnal.

It's fucking amazing.

We both moan each other's names as we reach our release.

Lowering her to her feet, I realize in our sexed-up frenzy, we were careless. "Fuuuuck," I groan, "we didn't use a condom."

Her eyes widen. "Shit. I'm on the pill and I've never not used protection before."

"Me neither."

We stare at each other nodding, and for the first time since we crossed that line it's silent and awkward between us. We each wash ourselves, not saying a word. Turning the water off, I hop out first and wrap a towel around my waist, grabbing another one, I unfold it and hold it open for Mia. She steps toward me and I wrap it around her, holding her in my arms. She rests her head on my chest and lets out a sigh, "Lawson—"

"Mia," I say, my tone harsher than I intended and it

causes her to lift her head. "Don't regret this, Mia because I sure as fuck don't. Last night was the best fucking night of my life."

"Mine too," she agrees with a smile, and that smile shoots straight to my heart. "Where do we go from here?" Her stomach rumbles and we both laugh.

"To breakfast, I guess," I tease in reply as my phone dings with a text from the other room. "I better get that."

She nods her head and reluctantly, I pull away from her and head into the room to check my message. Picking up my pants from last night, I dig out my phone and when I see who the message is from, I freeze. Staring back at me is a text from Travis. As I slide the button to unlock my phone, Mia's phone pings too, and I know that it will be from Travis too.

Sure enough, when I go to messages it's a group one.

TRAVIS: *Breakfast in 20*
LAWSON: *Roger that*

Looking up, I see Mia standing by the door wrapped in a towel, her clutch under her arm and her phone in her hand. Her eyes widen when she sees the message, then her fingers fly across the screen and then my phone pings.

MIA: *Pass*

She looks at me and shakes her head, "I can't face him yet, Lawson. I just can't." Her eyes well with tears and I see remorse written all over her face. "What if last night ruins everything between you guys?"

Shaking my head, I throw my phone on the bed and stalk over to her. Gripping her shoulders, she looks up at me. "No, Mia, no. Stop with the negative thoughts. I don't know what happens from here, but I do know I want to see where this goes."

"You do?" she questions, her voice laced with shock.

Nodding my head up and down, I smile at her. "I do, I really do." And that's the God's honest truth, I want to see where this goes. Mia and I have always gotten along and we have a sexual chemistry that's off the fucking charts.

"Okay...but I can't face Travis this morning. He'll know for sure."

"Fine. Can I see you later?"

With a smile, she nods. "I'd like that. How about you come over for dinner tonight?"

"I'd like that."

We nod at one another and then we each get dressed. Mia slips into her dress from last night, and I pull on a pair of cargos and a charcoal Henley. When I look up, I notice Mia staring at me. She smiles. "Guess I'll see you tonight."

"Yep," I reply, letting the 'P' pop.

She turns toward the door but immediately turns on her heel and walks over to me. She presses her lips to mine quickly before turning back around. The doors closes behind her, and I sit down on the end of the bed, shaking my head and smiling. I'm having dinner with Mia tonight.

Chapter Eleven

MIA

Leaning against the door to Lawson's room I grin; I slept with my brother's best friend last night, Oops!

Chapter Twelve

LAWSON

Flopping back to the mattress, I let out a sigh; I slept with my best friend's little sister last night, Oops!

Chapter Thirteen

MIA

Pushing off Lawson's door, I look both ways to make sure the coast is clear, and then I race down the hallway to my room. Stepping inside, I lean against the door and let out the breath I was holding as I snuck down the hotel hallway, like a teenager sneaking in waaaay after curfew on a Saturday night.

Sliding down to the floor, I lean my head back, close my eyes, and think about everything that happened last night. The kisses. The sex. The shower this morning. The sex, the amazing porn-worthy sex. It all vividly comes crashing back to me. I find myself grinning that my fantasy from when I was sixteen finally came true...and then fear sets in. I start to wonder if last night was the beginning of the end. What if Travis finds out? Did I just ruin their friendship by sleeping with my brother's best friend? Am I a friendship wrecker? A bad sister? *I'm a friendship wrecking whore.*

My phone beeps from my clutch. Pulling me from my friendship wrecker thoughts, I grab my phone and a smile breaks free when I see it's from Lawson. Swiping the message open, I read it.

LAWSON: *Stop overthinking things, everything will work out. See you 2nite **wink emoji***

How the hell did he know I was freaking out?

MIA: *I wasn't freaking out.*
LAWSON: *Liar liar pants on fire. I can hear your brain from here.*

I laugh at his reply and smile, it's crazy how well he knows me but then again, it's also not. We have known each other for years now, albeit through Travis. However, Lawson never treated me as 'Trav's lil' sister,' he's always treated me as 'Mia, the chick who always antagonizes her brother.'

MIA: *I wasn't freaking out.*
MIA: *Much*
LAWSON: *Don't make me spank you…unless you're into that*
MIA: *Maybe you'll find out tonight **wink wink***
MIA: *C U l8ter*

Dropping my phone to the carpet, I lean back against the door and sigh. Last night was beyond my wildest dreams. Never did I think I'd ever hook up with Lawson freakin O'Connor but I can unequivocally say, it was THE best night of my life. Now I just need to hope and pray it stays between us and that our night of unbridled passion doesn't throw a wrench in the works.

My phone pings again and I wonder what Lawson's reply to my last text will be. My eyes widen when I see it's from Trav.

TRAVIS: *Big nite, Sis?*

MIA: ***middle finger emoji***

TRAVIS: *Someone needs to get laid…thought you would have hooked up, being a bridesmaid and all that jazz*

LAWSON: *Yeah, Mia, thought you would have hooked up*

MIA: ***middle finger emoji***

SYDNEY: *Be nice, boys.*

MIA: *Yeah, be nice to sweet lil' old me*

TRAVIS: *Sweet my ass, dear sister of mine*

LAWSON: *Sweet ass **wink emoji***

LAWSON: *Come join us for breakfast? Pancakes are almost as good as sex*

TRAVIS: *Clearly you are fucking the wrong chicks if pancakes are as good as sex*

LAWSON: ***middle finger emoji***

TRAVIS: *Someone else clearly needs to get laid*

TRAVIS: *And why you winking at my sister????*

MIA: *As much as this is a riveting text chat, I'm going back to bed **middle finger emoji** **wink emoji** **sleeping emoji***

TRAVIS: *We are leaving at 12 sharp to head back, Sleeping Beauty.*
TRAVIS: *Don't be late*
MIA: *Yes, Dad*
MIA: *Good luck with D1 & D2, Syd*
SYDNEY: *You owe me **wine emoji***
LAWSON: *Nite nite, Sleeping Beauty. Sleep tight. Don't let the bed bugs bite.*
LAWSON: *See you two in 10…don't be late **wink emoji***

Shaking my head, I stand up and head into the room. Dropping my phone and clutch on the bedside table, I strip off my dress and bra, pull back the bed covers and climb in. I drift off to sleep, blissfully thinking about Lawson and what's going to happen next between us.

Chapter Fourteen

LAWSON

After our text chat finishes, I jump into the shower and images of Mia and me in here earlier flash though my mind. My cock hardens at the thought of her sexy as sin body. The water cascading down over her breasts and between her thighs. Gripping my cock in one hand, I place the other against the wall and I stroke. Imagining it's her hand and not mine, gripping and tugging my shaft. Sooner than I'd ever admit, I come, Mia's name slipping from my lips as I spray cum all over the shower wall.

Standing up straight, I let out a sigh and quickly get washed. Climbing out, I dry off, change back into my clothes, and head down to the restaurant where I find Travis and Sydney waiting for me. Syd waves and Trav gives me a head nod.

"Morning," I say, as I take a seat across from the love-birds, I look to the vacant seat beside me and really wish

Mia was here. It's amazing how in the last twelve hours she has overtaken my mind. I've been hanging around her for years and never really noticed her presence, or lack thereof, but this morning, she's noticeably absent and I miss her...dearly.

"Huh?" I say like a goofball when Trav kicks me under the table.

"Coffee, Sir?" the waitress asks me, lifting the pot in her hand for emphasis.

"Yes please," I say and she fills my mug. She offers a flirtatious smile. I smile back and nod my thanks. Then I add one sugar, since I'm not quite sweet enough.

"Dude, she totally was flirting with you."

"And?" I question, as I bring the mug to my lips and take a sip, my face scrunching up as the shitty coffee hits my taste buds. "Ugh, this tastes like ass."

"Can't say I've ever tasted ass, you, babe?" Sydney teases, as she takes a sip of her orange juice.

"No ass here," Trav teases.

"Fuck you both," I grumble, flipping them the bird as I stand up and head toward the buffet. Filling my plate with bacon, scrambled eggs, hash browns, and pancakes, I make my way back to the table to find Trav and Sydney making out like teenagers.

"Really? It's not even ten in the morning."

"You're just jealous that you don't have anyone to make out with before ten in the morning."

"Yeah, that's it," I retort with an eye roll for emphasis, and I pick up my coffee and take another shuddering sip.

"So, did you hook up last night?"

"Mi—"

Sydney interrupts me, "Babe, can you grab me my pancakes now, please?"

My eyes widen in shock. I can't believe I nearly said something to Travis about Mia and I hooking up last night. Thank God Sydney was here to save me and my balls and from the look in her eyes, I know that an intense conversation will be happening before we leave today. But what do I say to her? I really need to sort this out with Mia, whatever this is between us. I love Trav but after last night with Mia, it would be hard to choose between the two of them. Does that make me an asshole? There's that unwritten bros before hos code. But then again, I'm already in the asshole category because I fucked the one person in the world I shouldn't have, his sister...and it was fan-fucking-tubolous; I cannot wait to do it again. Yep, I'm an asshole.

Travis places a kiss on Sydney's cheek and goes to grab her pancakes. She looks over her shoulder and when she sees that Trav is out of earshot, she turns to me. "Are you a complete moron? Did Mia fuck your brains out last night or something?"

My eyes widen at her. "How did you know?"

"Please, you two were all over each other last night. And you've been eye-fucking her ever since Tayla and Corbin's wedding a few weeks ago."

"Does Travis know?"

"You're still alive," she pointedly says.

"Fair point," I sigh. "Do you think he'll kill me?"

"You're fucking his little sister, what do you think?"

"It's more than fucking, Syd," I say, shocking myself,

and clearly surprising Sydney too, because her mouth is wide open.

"Explain?"

"I can't really, but all I know is I can't stop thinking about her and last night. Last night was more than just fucking, I think it might have been the start of something...more. As long as Travis doesn't kill me, that is."

"You guys need to figure it out, but most of all, don't hide it. Secrets never stay hidden. For what it's worth, I hope you two figure it out because you are perfect for each other."

"Whose perfect for each other?" Travis says, as he places the biggest stack of pancakes down in front of Sydney.

Without missing a beat she says, "Raine and Jenson. If two people are meant to be together, it's them, and just think," she turns her gaze to me, "if they'd been honest from the start, it wouldn't have taken them this long to finally become man and wife."

"Damn fucking right. Luckily, I got it right without any hiccups."

"You sure did, Babycakes," Sydney dreamily says to him and then they make out.

Leaning back in my chair, I think about what Sydney said and she's right. Mia and I need to figure this out because keeping secrets will only lead to issues, and we don't want any trouble, but I think last night may have already opened that door. Oops.

Chapter Fifteen

MIA

THE LASAGNA IS IN THE OVEN BAKING. THE SALAD IS ready and the garlic bread is waiting on the stovetop. Now I just need Lawson to arrive and the evening can get underway. Pouring myself a glass of wine, I walk into the living room and take a seat on the sofa. It's the first time I've stopped since getting home. As I sip on my wine, I think about the last twenty-four hours. I have to pinch myself to confirm I'm awake because this feels like a dream, a fucking amazing dream. I slept with Lawson O'Connor and I can say, it's far better than I ever imagined, but now I have so many questions.

How the hell did we get here?

What's going to happen next?

What if Travis finds out? He looks good in orange but not sure he could pull off jumpsuit orange, because when he finds out that his best friend slept with me, Lawson is a dead man.

And where does that leave us? I don't want this to just be a drunken wedding hookup. I want it all with Lawson, but can we?

Chugging back my wine, I place the empty glass on the coffee table, lean back on the sofa and sigh, my wallowing is interrupted by a knock at the front door. My head snaps up and I smile, my heart races because of who is on the other side of the door. Jumping up, I bang my knee on the edge of the coffee table. "Motherfucker," I groan, as I limp toward the door. Swinging it open, all thoughts of the pain in my knee disappear when my eyes land on Lawson. Holy sex on a stick, this man is pure perfection.

"Hey," he croons, as his eyes rake over my body. My skin heating from the intensity of his gaze. I'm wearing a spaghetti strap navy dress that fits me like a glove and accentuates the girls.

"Hey," I reply, as my eyes once again roam over him. He's wearing dark denim jeans that I know will be hugging is ass perfectly, a black Henley, and his aviators.

"My eyes are up here, Mia."

Lifting my gaze to his, my cheeks darken. We stare at one another, it's heated and carnal but the moment is interrupted when the timer on the oven beeps. It takes each of us a few moments to move. Taking a few steps, I look over my shoulder. "You coming?"

"You will be soon," he boldly replies and steps inside, closing the door behind him as he follows me into the kitchen.

Bending down, I take the lasagna out and pop the

garlic bread in. "Hope you're hungry." I say, feeling nervous all of a sudden.

"I'm famished," he says. "Wine?" He lifts up a bottle of red.

Nodding I turn and reach up to grab two wine glasses. Lawson steps behind me, his chest pressing into my back. I close my eyes and enjoy the feeling of his body against mine. I can feel his breath on my neck. Turning to face him, we stare intently at one another. Licking my bottom lip, I wish for him to kiss me. He leans forward but he doesn't. Instead he grabs the wine glasses and steps back to the counter, leaving me a wanton, panting mess. Grabbing the corkscrew from the draw, I hand it to him and when our fingers brush, an electrical current zaps between us. Swallowing deeply, I turn around to the stove, needing a few moments to calm down. This is new territory for us, I'm both scared and excited for what's possibly going to happen.

I feel Lawson behind me and spin to face him, he was closer than I expected and I knock the glass of wine in his hand. He's covered in red wine, as is the floor. "Ohh shit-balls, I'm so sorry."

"It's fine," he replies, placing the almost empty glass onto the countertop. He reaches behind his head and in that sexy way that guys do, he grabs the neck of his shirt and pulls it over his head. Dropping down, he uses his shirt to wipe up the mess.

"Lawson," I scoff, "Don't use your shirt."

"It's fine, it was all messed up anyway."

"Mmmhmpf," I say, my eyes raking over his chest as he stands up and drops the soiled shirt into the sink.

"Mia, if you continue to look at me like that, I will have no choice but to bend you over this counter and have my way with you."

"I'm okay with that." Turning around, I turn the oven off. Looking back to Lawson, I purse my lips and then think, *Fuck it.* Stepping to him, I grip his cheeks and cover his mouth with mine. He pushes his tongue into my mouth and takes over the kiss. He taps my ass and I jump into his arms, then he turns around and stalks down the hallway to my bedroom.

Dropping me to the bed, I sit and stare up at him. My hands lift on their own accord and I make quick work of stripping him out of his jeans. He kicks them and his shoes off and when he stands back up, I lean forward and swipe my tongue across the head of his cock. Opening my mouth, I slide his cock between my lips and suck, the head hitting the back of my throat.

"Mia," he moans. Threading his hands into my hair, he pulls me off and stares down at me. "I want to taste you too."

Shuffling back on the bed, I lift my dress over my head, leaving me in only my panties. "Fuck me, Mia, you are stunning."

"And you are still standing at the end of my bed. I want your cock in my mouth and your tongue in my pussy." I pause. "Now!"

"Yes, ma'am." He winks at me and my body comes alive with that action.

Lawson turns around, sits on the edge of my bed, and lies back. He stares back at me and raises his eyebrows suggestively. Returning the action, I lift to my knees, lean down, and kiss him deeply before I continue down his body. My head hovers above his cock and I'm now straddling his head. He grips my hips and pulls me down onto his face. He attacks me in the most pleasurable way, my eyes droop closed, and I give myself over to him. Dropping my head, his cock pokes my cheek and I remember I'm supposed to be sucking him.

Opening wide I suck him into my mouth and lift my hand to squeeze the base of his shaft. He groans and sucks my clit into his mouth, causing me to moan around his cock. Sliding his shaft in and out of my mouth, I focus on him but it's getting hard—pun intended—because he is devouring me as if he's a starved man.

His cock twitches and I know he's close. I am too, my body is zinging. Lawson presses his finger against my butthole and I explode. I scream around his cock as I come, my body thrumming in the most pleasurable way. A few seconds later, Lawson comes with a guttural groan. I suck him dry and then roll off of him. We both lie on my bed, panting and breathing heavily.

The perfect moment is interrupted when my stomach growls. We both laugh, and then Lawson's stomach growls in reply to mine.

"Guess we should eat now," I say, as I sit up and stare over at him.

"Best appetizer I've ever had," he replies with a wink.

Rolling my eyes, I shake my head and stand up. Grabbing my dress, I pull it over my head. "I'll go dish up."

Walking out of my room, I head to the kitchen with a smile on my face.

Chapter Sixteen

LAWSON

WELL THIS WASN'T HOW I PLANNED ON THE EVENING going but I can say, it's off to a banging start. Pulling on my jeans, I head out and join Mia. We are both quiet as she dishes up dinner. I pour us more wine and place the glasses on the dining table—without spilling or wearing any this time.

Mia places our plates on the table and we both sit. We eat in silence for a few moments, it's awkward, really awkward. I knew the awkwardness would appear but I was also kinda hoping it wouldn't. On the drive back today, I decided I want to see where this goes with Mia. I don't want this to be a one, well, two-time thing.

Lifting my wine, a take a sip and look up to see Mia watching me over the rim of her wine glass. "Sooo—"

"Buttons," she replies and we both laugh, she and I do this all the time. She'll say, 'Hey' and I'll reply with, 'Is for horses.' Or 'Well' and the other replies, with 'that's a pretty deep subject.' And if it happens to be Travis who says well, the other will tack on 'for such a shallow mind.' He hates when we do that.

"Mia, I..."

"You what?"

"I want more. I want to see where this goes."

"Really?" Her eyebrows shoot up in shock.

"Really, really. Mia, this wasn't just some random wedding hookup to me. I'm hoping it's the start of something amazing."

"Really?" she questions again.

"Really, really."

"Stop with the *Shrek* references."

"Sorry, but it's true." Reaching over, I take her hand in mine. "Mia, what happened between us was totally out of the blue, but I don't regret it at all. I want you more than I have ever wanted someone before."

"Lawson, I've wanted this for as long as I can remember." I smirk because everyone knew about her crush on me. She rolls her eyes but goes on, "I keep thinking I'm going to wake up from the best dream ever." She pauses and bites her lip. "I'm scared, Law."

"About?"

"Ruining things."

"What could you possibly ruin?"

"Yours and Travis's relationship. My relationship with him."

"Take him out of the picture, what else is holding you back?"

"Nothing else. I like you Lawson, like really, really like you."

"Now who's Shreking who?"

She sticks out her tongue at me and bites her bottom lip again, and I really want to suck and bite her lip. "Where do we go from here?"

"Back to bed." I confidently reply, this gets me another eye roll from Mia. "But seriously, Mia, let's take it one day at a time." She nods her head but she's still not convinced. "What if we keep it between us, for now? Once we know what we have is permanent, then we can tell people."

"You'd do that?"

Nodding my head, I reach over and take her hand. "Mia, if it means I can be with you, then yes." Lifting our joined hands to my lips, I kiss her knuckles, hoping the gesture will reassure her. "Mia, will you secretly date me until we know what exactly is going on between us?"

She nods her head eagerly and smiles. "Yes, Lawson, I will secretly date you until we know what exactly is going on between us." She takes a deep breath. "What do you think Travis will do when he finds out?"

"One of two things. One, he accepts us willingly, or two, I'll be six feet under and he'll be rocking an orange jumpsuit for the next twenty-five years to life."

"I really hope it's option one."

"Me too, babe, me too." Her grins widens. "Why are you grinning like you just won *Mario Kart*?"

"You called me babe, I used to get so jealous when you'd call your previous girlfriends babe. Never in a million years did I think I'd hear *you* call *me* babe."

"Well, babe, how about we head to the bedroom and I can have you for dessert?"

"Babe, would very much like that."

"Then let's go."

Taking Mia's hand, I walk us into her bedroom where I feast on her for dessert and then we make love: sweet, sweet love.

Chapter Seventeen

MIA

Oops, I slept with my brother's best friend again.

Chapter Eighteen

LAWSON

Oops, I slept with my best friend's little sister again.

Chapter Nineteen

MIA

The last few weeks sneaking around with Lawson have been amazing, beyond amazing. Better than my wildest dreams could have ever imagined. I'd often wondered if I'd put him up on a pedestal, but spending one-on-one time with him has proved to me he really is the perfect guy.

There has only been one occasion when we were nearly busted. We were at Trav and Sydney's finalizing wedding stuff. They were both out of the room and I couldn't control myself. I pushed him into the pantry and attacked him. Slamming my lips to his in an all consuming NSFP kiss, no sooner did we exit the pantry and Syd returned. The look she gave me indicated she knew something happened, but Travis came back and saved me from her questions. I have to say, sneaking around has been fun and it's bonded us together in a much deeper way.

Lawson and I have really clicked as a couple. I just wish we could sing it from the rooftops because I'm falling head over heels for my brother's best friend. This weekend is going to be tough, hiding how I really feel, but this weekend is all about Travis and Sydney, their wedding weekend is finally here. Since Law and I are both in the bridal party, we are going to be in close proximity twenty-four seven, it will be hard to not touch or kiss him whenever I want. I think I need to broach the subject of us coming out as a couple, but after this weekend. I don't want anything to ruin my big brother's wedding.

The sound of my brother's voice snaps me back to the present, "The rules are simple, you follow the clues and the first team back here with all the scavenger hunt items wins."

"What's the prize?" Jensen and Raine both yell out at the same time, then they lovingly look at one another. Lawson pretends to vomit at their lovey-doveyness. I jab him in the ribs; he just shrugs and laughs.

"Now that there, is a love." Trav says. "Lawson, you'll have a love like that one day."

"Poor girl," Jensen teases. Everyone laughs. Lawson just shakes his head, flips Jensen the bird, and when he looks back at me, he winks. My insides turn to jelly at the gesture.

"...and the prize is a one hundred dollar bar voucher to be used this weekend." A murmuring of approval erupts within the group. "Now, since most of us are here in couples, we will stick with that. Sorry, Lawson, you're stuck with my sister since you two are the only single ones."

"Screw you, Big Brother," I scoff and flip him the bird.

Lawson throws his arm around my shoulder, looks to Trav, and says, "Game on, asshole. Mia and I are gonna smash this." He then turns his gaze and stares at me. The intensity of his stare is smoldering. "We got this, babe," he says, placing a kiss on my temple.

There's that word again, 'babe.' I don't think I'll ever get used to hearing him say that. At the same time, I hope I get to hear it forever.

Hearing Travis shout, "And go!" snaps me back to the present, I didn't even realize Syd handed Lawson an envelope with the first clue. Lawson takes my hand and pulls me over to the fireplace. He drops my hand and rips open the envelope and reads. Without saying a word, he takes my hand again and drags me out of the bar.

"Good luck with that dead weight!" Travis yells, garnering himself a smack in the arm from Sydney and a flip of the bird from both Lawson and me.

Twenty minutes later, we are still searching for the first clue's answer. Lawson and I suck but we are having a blast, laughing our asses off. We have nooooo fucking clue where we should be looking. Every time we think we have it, we are proven wrong. Sitting down in one of the cabanas by the pool, I sigh, "We are totally gonna to lose."

"We sure are, BUUUUUT I cannot think of a better person to lose with," Lawson says, staring down at me.

"Aww, you say the sweetest things sometimes," I reply as I stare up at him.

We gaze at one another, the air around us thickens. Lawson steps to me, cups my cheeks in his palms, leans down and presses his lips to mine. Closing my eyes, I lose myself in Lawson and the kiss. Draping my arms over his shoulders, I pull him to me. We begin to fall back to the cabana mattress when Lawson is pulled away from me.

Chapter Twenty

LAWSON

"Wʜᴀᴛ ᴛʜᴇ ғᴜᴄᴋ?" Tʀᴀᴠɪs ɢʀᴏᴡʟs, ᴀs ʜᴇ viciously pulls me away from Mia. He's fuming. Clenching his fists and breathing like a bull. If we were in a cartoon, his face would be beet red and steam would be billowing out of his ears; I'm fucked. "Why the fuck are you kissing my sister?" he snarls through clenched teeth, his eyes shooting daggers at me.

"Travis," Mia says, as she stands up and steps toward her brother. "It's—"

"Shut the fuck up, Mia, I'm talking to him." He stabs his finger into my chest, the vein in his forehead pulsing as his anger builds.

"Hey, man, don't speak to her like that."

"Shut the fuck up, Lawson, I'll speak to my sister however the fuck I want."

The three of us fall silent. The air around us simmering with animosity and angst. Mia looks like she's ready to burst into tears and Travis looks like he wants to kill me.

"Trav," Mia timidly says, she sounds so broken right now. She swallows deeply. "We can explain."

"Well, fucking do it," he spits, clenching and unclenching his fists in anger.

Stepping in front of Mia, I warn, "Travis, you have a problem with me, not her."

"Damn fucking right I have a fucking problem. You were just mouth-fucking my sister." He shoves me in the chest, "What the fuck, man?"

"Travis," Sydney scolds as she joins us. "What are you doing? What's going on?" Her gaze darts between the three of us with concern.

"I just caught these two making out."

"So?" Sydney asks, her eyes flicking to Travis.

"So," Travis growls. "So? He was kissing my fucking sister."

"So? I kiss you all the time."

"He was kissing my sister," Trav snarls again, "My fucking sister."

"Did you maybe think she wants him to be kissing her? Did you maybe think for the last few weeks they have been getting closer? Did you think at all before you went all big brother caveman asshole?" My gaze snaps to Sydney's at this revelation, she shakes her head and her lips lift into a smirk. "Guys, a blind man could see what's been happening between you two."

"You knew?" Trav and Mia say at the same time.

"Well, yeah," she nonchalantly says, shrugging her shoulders.

"Why didn't you say anything to me?" Travis snaps.

"Because I knew you'd act like a dick."

"A big one," I add, but it was a mistake because Travis raises his arm and his fist flies at my face. His knuckles collide with my cheekbone. My head snaps toward Mia and I stumble back onto the cabana mattress. Her eyes are wide and filled with tears, this is her worst fear coming true.

"Mia," I say as I stand up. "Mia, babe, look at me?" She turns her head to me and my heart breaks at the devastation etched on her face right now. "This doesn't change anything," I plead.

"Like fuck it doesn't," Travis says, stepping between Mia and me, pushing her away from me. "You stay the fuck away from my sister."

Shaking my head, I stare at Mia behind him. "Sorry, man, I can't. I—"

"No," Mia shouts. Stepping around Travis, she places her hand on my cheek, I lean into it and smile at her. "Don't finish that sentence Lawson," she cries, "this was... it's a...I'm sorry...I...I—" She turns around and runs away from us in tears.

Spinning around, I yell out but she keeps running. Travis grabs my arm, halting me. Looking back at him over my shoulder, I shake my head. Turning back around, I watch Mia run away from me. My heart is breaking and then it hits me, the woman I love just ran away from me.

Turning back to Travis and Sydney, I see rage all over his face. "You are dead to me, Lawson O'Connor. Fucking dead to me." He turns around and storms away, kicking a trash can as he heads back inside the hotel.

In the space of two minutes, I lost the woman I love—yes love—and my best friend. "Fuuuuck!" I growl, running my fingers through my hair, staring at the ground.

"Lawson," Sydney says, "look at me." Lifting my gaze to hers I see pain reflecting back at me. "If you really love her like I think you do, he'll come around."

"How do you know that?"

"Because he wants you both to be happy." She steps to me and squeezes my shoulder. "But do you think you could have waited until after the wedding to declare your love for her? You knew this was how he would react, hence the sneaking around."

"How did you know?"

"I'm a woman about to get married, love is in my veins and in the air right now. Plus I've seen how you two look at one another, ever since Raine and Jensen's wedding. You two have both been different AND you both eye-fuck the hell out of each other when you think no one is watching."

Shaking my head, I laugh. "Well, how did he not see?"

"Dude, you've met your best friend? He's not the sharpest tool in the shed when it comes to love. Look how long it took him to realize I wanted to date him."

"True." I nod in agreement. "How do I fix this?"

"Give him time. I guarantee you, by the rehearsal dinner tonight, everything will be fixed."

"How can you be so confident?"

"Because love is in the air."

"I wish I was as optimistic as you are."

"I have to be, I'm getting married this weekend. And even though my soon-to-be husband is being an irrational jackass right now, I know that deep down, he knew this was coming. He just doesn't want to lose you or Mia."

"He won't."

"Well, you need to make him see that."

"Thanks, Syd." I pull her in for a hug. "Sorry to have ruined everything."

She pulls back and smiles. "The only way that this will be ruined, is if I don't walk down the aisle tomorrow and say I do."

"I won't let that happen."

"Good," she says. "Now, go win over your girl and I'll deal with your jackass of a best friend." With that she turns and walks away from me. Plonking down to the cabana mattress, I stare up at the sky. I need to come up with a plan to win back the trust of my best friend and convince Mia I'm worth it. That *we* are worth it.

Standing up, I walk inside and it hits me, much like Travis' fist: I'm head over heels, ass over tit, in love with my best friend's little sister, Oops!

Chapter Twenty One

MIA

With tears pouring down my face, I race through the lobby, down the corridor, and head to my room, ever so grateful to have a ground floor room. Unlocking my door, I step inside and throw myself onto the bed. Tears cascade down my cheeks and I let it all out. My fear of ruining Travis and Lawson's friendship has come true. "I'm the worst person ever," I cry to the empty room.

Standing up, I walk over to the mini bar and I even though this mini bottle of vodka is going to cost me a gazillion dollars, I twist the cap off and chug it back. It burns like a mofo but I deserve it. By giving into my desires, I just cost my brother and his best friend their friendship. Grabbing the other mini vodka, I go to twist off the top when a knock at the door freezes me. I don't want to see anyone at the moment. I need to wallow alone and mourn the loss of my brother and Lawson's relationship, and for the fact I've lost Lawson too. At the thought of losing Lawson, I cover my mouth, drop to my knees, and a guttural sob breaks free.

"Let me in," Sydney says, as she knocks again.

It's Syd, yeah, I can see her. I want to see her. Standing up, I walk over to the door and open it. "Ohh, Mia," she coos, enveloping me in a hug. Wrapping my arms around her, I cry into her shoulder. Sobbing my broken heart out.

"Syd, I've ruined everything," I blubber.

"No you haven't," she says, gripping my cheeks in her palm. She brushes a tendril of hair behind my ear. "Your brother was just taken by surprise. When he realizes how much of a dick he was, he'll come apologize." I eye her. "Okay, we'll need to spell it out for him, but he *will* come around, Mia. Trust me."

"Ma'am," someone from the hall says, "I have your room service order."

"I didn't order anything."

"I did," Syd says. Grinning at me, she pushes me into my room and holds the door open for the attendant. He drops off the cart and exits my room.

Sydney grabs the bottle of bubbly from the wine bucket, pops the cork, fills up two champagne flutes, and hands one to me. She grabs the cheese board, her bubbly and sits cross legged on my bed and she takes a sip. "Okay, tell me everything."

For the next ten minutes I fill her in on everything that's happened between Lawson and me since the night of Raine and Jensen's wedding. She's looking at me with hearts in her eyes, she really is a big romantic.

"Ohh, Mia, I am so happy for you both."

"Yeah, but now, nothing more can happen."

"Why not?" she asks, hopping up to refill our now empty flutes. She hands mine back to me. "Give me one good reason why you and Lawson cannot be together, and don't even think about using your stupid brother as an excuse."

"You just referred to your fiancé, my brother, as stupid. Your fiancé whom you are marrying tomorrow."

"If he acts stupid, I'll call him stupid and right now, he's the biggest stupid head there is. So what, his best friend and sister hooked up, it's not like you killed anyone." She pauses. "You haven't killed anyone have you?" Shaking my head no, she continues, "The heart wants what the heart wants, screw everyone else."

"But—"

"No buts, Mia Grace Templeton."

"You must be serious, you full named me."

Sydney ignores me and continues on with her speech, "I've always seen a spark between you and him. It was inevitable this would happen and now that it has; don't let it go. Hold on with both hands and fight. You fight hard for the one you love. Mia, everyone deserves love and to be loved."

"But what about their friendship?"

"It will be fine. They, meaning Travis, will be a big stupid butthead for a bit, but once he's calmed down and sees this rationally, he'll be happy for you both."

"God, I hope so, Syd, because I really like Lawson."

"I know you do, and that's why everything will work out. From what you've told me, this isn't just some fling between you two. Mia, you are a girl who's in love with her big brother's best friend, which so happens to sound like an epic love if you ask me."

I let those words sink in and she finishes her bubbly. Placing the empty glass on the side table, she hops up. "The rehearsal dinner starts in an hour, I expect to see you there." Placing a kiss on my forehead, she turns and leaves to get ready.

Letting out a sigh, I finish off my drink, stand up, and walk into the bathroom. As I look at my reflection in the mirror, I smile for the first time since shit hit the fan. Sydney is right, I'm hopelessly in love with my big brother's best friend. Oops!

Chapter Twenty Two

LAWSON

Well, fuck me sideways, this wasn't how I imagined Travis finding out about Mia and me. And I really didn't expect him to punch me, but then again, he did find me making out with his sister, at least we weren't fucking. I think he would have murdered me if he found us doing the naked horizontal tango. Taking a seat at the bar, I ask for some ice, a tea towel, and a beer. The beer is placed in front of me and I pick it up. I chug back half the bottle, the yeasty goodness helping me relax. When the ice and towel are dropped off, I order another beer. Popping some ice into the towel, I lift it to my eye. "Motherfucker," I groan.

"Language, Lawson O'Connor." Turning my head, I see Grace Templeton walking toward me, she eyes the cloth and her mouth drops. "I take it Travis found out about you and Mia?"

"How the f—how did you know?"

"Please, I'm a mother," she says with a roll of her eyes. "A glass of Shiraz and a scotch, please," she asks the bartender, and then turns her attention back to me. "Lawson, dear, I've seen the way Mia has looked at you since she was ten years old. In the last few weeks, when you thought no one was looking, you had the exact same gaze and sparkle in your eyes too."

"Well, we're over now." She eyes me. "If Travis has his way, we will be."

"And what do you want?" she asks, as the barman places her drinks on the bar top.

"Mia," I say without missing a beat.

"Then screw what my son thinks and follow your heart. Swoop my daughter off her feet and love her the way she deserves to be loved."

Nodding my head, I watch her walk over to Garrett. He takes the scotch from her and kisses her cheek as she sits down. I want that, I want a love like Mr. and Mrs. Templeton. I know Mia and I can have that. I just need to convince Mia we are meant to be and then get Travis on board. Easy, right?

Chapter Twenty Three

MIA

Everyone is in the private dining room for the rehearsal dinner, everyone except Lawson that is. My eyes keep drifting toward the entrance, hoping to see him, but he's yet to arrive. Travis keeps glaring at me; clearly he's still angry about this afternoon. I want to talk to him but I don't want to ruin this for Sydney, and him; even though he's acting like a huge jerk face jackass.

Mom and Dad come over and they each hug me hello, I haven't seen them yet since I was hiding out in my room after the scavenger hunt debacle. Mom is talking about wedding stuff but I'm not really listening. The hairs on the back of my neck prickle and I know he's here. Turning around, my eyes lock on his as he steps through the door. Holy crap on a cracker, Lawson is hot tonight. Black dress pants, navy dress shirt with the top buttons undone. His hair is styled in that perfectly imperfect messy way. I want to run my finger through it, just to mess it up a little and annoy him.

He's walking toward us, his eyes are locked on mine. He's a few steps from us when Travis bellows, "O'Connor, get the fuck out!" He steps in front of me, blocking me from Lawson.

"No," Lawson defiantly says to Trav. His gaze steadfastly locked on my brother.

"Trav," I say, resting my hand on his shoulder.

"This doesn't concern you, Mia," he spits. "This is between me and my ex-best friend."

"No," I whisper as my eyes well with tears, I shake my head from side to side. All my fears are now confirmed, me being with Lawson has ended their friendship.

"Travis," I hear Lawson say, "I don't want to fight you, or lose you, but Mia and I, we are happening whether you like it or not."

"Over my dead body. You will never touch my sister again."

"Don't you think that's up to her?"

"No, she doesn't know what she wants."

"Excuse me?" I say, smacking my brother up the back of the head, he turns to face me. He's fuming. "You don't control me, Travis Nathaniel Templeton. You don't dictate who I kiss and you certainly do not tell me what to do."

"Watch me. This is just a wedding hookup, nothing more."

"You don't know shit, man," Lawson says.

"Shut your fucking mouth, O'Connor."

"No, Travis, no. Any other time, I'd step aside but not this time." His gaze gravitates to me, a force takes over my body and I step around Trav. I gaze into Lawson's eyes and smile, my heart starts rapidly beating when he takes my hand in his and squeezes.

"Mia, I love you. I didn't realize how deeply I did, until you walked away from me earlier. I couldn't breathe, my heart literally stopped beating in my chest with each step you took away from me. I'd give up everything to have you by my side, Mia, *everything*." His words register and I realize he's choosing me.

Cupping his cheek in my palm, I grin. "I love you too, Lawson. I've loved you since I was ten years old. This afternoon has been hell. Not knowing what was going to happen with us, or with Trav, was killing me, but as soon as I saw you just now, I knew. I knew I loved you and that it'll all be okay."

We stare at one another. Everyone is watching us right now but I don't give a flying fuck. Lawson just admitted he loves me and I love him, that's all I care about.

"For fuck's sake," Jensen groans, "just kiss already."

"With pleasure." Lawson steps me to, grips my cheeks in his palms, and presses his lips to mine. Closing my eyes, I give everything I have to this kiss. I lose myself in everything that is Lawson O'Connor, everything and everyone fades into the background.

"Stop, just fucking stop," Travis interrupts.

"Travis Nathaniel Templeton," Dad growls, "you need to back up, tone it down, and leave your sister alone."

"But—"

"But nothing, Son, your sister and Lawson are together. You need to find a way to accept it."

Travis purses his lips and sighs. His gaze flicks between Lawson and me, a look washes over him but I can't read him. He's really good at hiding his emotions. His lips lift in a slight grin and I know he's going to give us a chance. Stepping out from under Lawson's arm, I stop in front of Trav. "You sure, Big Brother?"

"Yeah, I'm sure." He looks to Syd and winks. "A wise woman once told me, that when you find 'the one,' you hold on with both hands and fight. You fight hard for the one you love and screw the dickhead big brother." We all laugh, "I really am sorry I acted like a dick."

"We're used to it," Lawson and I say in unison.

"You two really are the perfect pair." He pauses and stares at Lawson. "You hurt her, and I'll fucking kill you."

"I have no doubt that you would, but I promise I won't give you a reason to because I love her too much to ever let her go."

Chapter Twenty Four

MIA

...twelve months later

We are back at the resort where Sydney and Travis got married last year, they are having an anniversary weekend. *Fucking weirdos*, I'd be spending my anniversary with my husband, naked and fucking like rabbits, but each to their own I guess.

"You realize that when we get married you'll become Mia O'Connor." I look at Lawson blankly, I have no fucking clue what he's going on about right now. "Like from *Fast and Furious?*"

"You think about us getting married?"

"Yeah, don't you?"

"Well, yeah, but I'm a girl. Aren't you worried about Trav killing you?"

"Not when it comes to you, besides I could totally take him."

"If you say so."

"Are you doubting my abilities as a man?"

"Don't go putting words in my mouth...I'd rather put something else in my mouth."

We silently stare at one another for a few beats and then he grabs my hand, laces our fingers, and drags me back to our room.

The door clicks shut behind us and we rip off our clothes as we walk into the room. By the time we reach the bed, we are both naked as the day we were born. Lawson raises his eyebrows at me, I wink and drop to my knees. With my eyes locked on his, I gently stroke his cock up and down. The top glistening with precum. Darting my tongue out, I swipe the tip over the head of his cock before taking his shaft into my mouth and sucking.

"Fuuuuck!" Lawson growls, threading his fingers into my golden locks. "I love the way you suck my cock," he says, as he guides my head up and down. Lifting my hand, I cup and squeeze his balls, he hisses above me and I know he's close. Lifting up, I slide his cock between my breasts and sandwich his cock between them. His eyes pop open and he looks down to see his cock sliding between my breasts. "Fuck me, Mia. That's hotter than seeing my cock between your lips."

That's what you think, I think to myself. On the next slide, I lower my head down and suck the head of his cock before sliding it back down and between my breasts. Looking up, I see that he's closed his eyes again. He scrunches his face and with a guttural roar, he comes.

The first spurt sprays my chest and neck. Sliding his cock into my mouth, I lick and suck him until he's finished.

Standing up, I swipe my finger through the cum on my chest and seductively suck my finger. Lying back on the bed, I shuffle up to the pillows and open my legs. I'm soaked and ready for him to fuck me. Lawson stares down at me, his gaze heated and carnal. Grabbing my ankles, he pulls me down the bed, drops to his knees and licks me from taint to clit. "Fuuuuck!" I moan, grabbing my breasts and squeezing them as he continues to devour me with his tongue. He slips the tip of his pinky into my ass, and its sets off a series of explosions. I come harder than ever before, soaking his face and the bed...and quite possibly the room below us.

"Fuck me," I pant, lifting my arm, I cover my eyes, trying to control my breathing.

"If you insist," Lawson says, lying down next to me.

Rolling to my side, I snuggle into him. "Just, give me a few." He laughs but wraps his arm around me, pulling me into him farther. Placing a kiss on my forehead, he whispers, "Marry me?"

My head snaps up and I see him staring intently at me. "Come again?"

"Marry me, Mia Templeton? I want you to become my wife, I want you to be Mrs. Mia O'Connor. You are my everything, be my forever, Mia. Marry me?"

Shifting to my knees, I stare down at him. "Yes, yes, I'll marry you. I'll be your everything because, Lawson, you are my everything."

Opening the drawer on the bedside table, he pulls out a velvet box. Flicking it open, I see the most gorgeous ring

I have ever seen. A tear drop diamond, sits on a rose gold band. He pulls the ring out, shuffles to his knees, takes my left hand, and slides it onto my ring finger.

Lifting my hand up, I wriggle my fingers and smile. "I love you, Lawson, and I cannot wait to become your wife."

"I love you too, Mia, and I cannot wait to be your husband."

We collapse onto the bed and cement our union. As I drift off to sleep in my fiancé's arms, I smile. I'm going to marry my big brother's best friend. Oops...nah, I say fuck yeah!

Epilogue

MIA

Finally the bride and not the bridesmaid.

My friends can no longer tease me because today is MY wedding day. Today I'm the bride. Today I will marry my childhood crush, Lawson O'Connor. I have dreamed of this day since I was ten years old. I finally get the white dress, the fancy reception, and the husband of my dreams. Little does everyone know that technically I already am Mrs. Mia O'Connor; Oops. You see, three weeks ago, while we were in Vegas for a conference with work, we eloped. Even though today was booked, we didn't want to wait another moment to become man and wife, so we did it. We got hitched. My mind drifts back to that magical time...

...The sales conference was batshit boring, as it usually was but thankfully this year, it was in Vegas and Lawson

joined me on the last night. I extended my stay so he and I could have a getaway before our big day. We will be having a fun dirty weekend before we head into the final crazy few weeks before our wedding.

We spent the first day after the conference lazy by the pool, and then we spent the evening in our room, eating room service and fucking like rabbits. Today we explored the strip and when we got back to the hotel, we stopped in the casino for a little gambling. We left with an extra two grand in our pocket so we decided to treat ourselves. Tonight we were going to go to Gordon Ramsay Steak located within the Paris Hotel. The prices were outrageous but we won two grand and it was our last hurrah, so why not.

Slipping into a chocolate brown halter dress, I headed out to meet Lawson. I paused midstep, man, my fiancé was hot. When he spun around to face me, his eyes raked over my body. My skin tingled at the intensity in his gaze. "You are fucking gorgeous, Mia."

"You're not too bad yourself there, Mr. Lawson. Now take me to dinner so I can replenish my energy levels, because we are going to need it for what I have in mind when we get back."

"I like the way you think. Let's go."

Sliding his hand around my waist, we exited the room and headed toward the restaurant. I loved that everything was in walking distance in Vegas. After the most amazing steak I ever had in my life, we headed to the Bellagio Fountains, seeing it with someone you love, made it so much better than seeing it by yourself. We stopped in at a cocktail bar on our way back to our hotel. The atmosphere *was electric and before I knew it, Lawson and I were two sheets to the wind, laughing at everything and making out like teenagers.*

Blurry eyed, I looked to Lawson and smiled. He glanced up and caught me staring at him. "What?"

"Nothing." I shook my head. "I'm just happy and I cannot wait to marry you."

We stared at one another. Everything around us faded away. It was just the two of us.

"Let's get married," he said, breaking our stare off.

"We are, in three weeks' time."

He shook his head. "No, now. Let's get hitched. Tonight."

"Really?"

"Really, really."

Staring at him, I processed his words. Biting my bottom lip, I contemplated it and with a grin, I nodded. "Why the fuck not. Let's do it. Let's get hitched."

He wrapped his arms around my waist, lifted me up, and spun us around. He pressed his lips to mine. Then pulled back. "Are you sure?"

I nodded my head. "I'm positive. I've never been more sure of anything. I've wanted this forever and I cannot wait to become Mrs. Mia O'Connor."

"Finally like Fast and Furious."

"And I cannot wait to ride you...all night long."

He pressed his lips to mine again and then whispered, "I can't wait to do all the dirty sexy things to my wife."

"You and me both."

He threw his head back and yelled, "We're getting married tonight!"

The entire cocktail bar erupted into cheers and whistles. Lawson placed me back on my feet and dragged me out of the bar. We climbed into a taxi. "To a chapel," he told the driver, then turned his attention to me. "Are you sure?"

Again I nodded my head. "I've never been more sure of anything. I've wanted this forever and I cannot wait to become Mrs. Mia O'Connor."

"Like Fast and Furious," the driver says.

"Exactly like that," I say.

We pulled up outside A Chapel of Love and headed in. We were greeted by a lovely older lady and ninety minutes later, I was officially Mrs. Mia O'Connor.

We made our way back to the hotel, ordered champagne from room service, and cemented our union as husband and wife...

My happy memory is interrupted by a knock at the door. "Come in!" I shout, and when he door swings opens, I smile. "Lawson, you can't see the bride before the ceremony, it's bad luck."

"Well, you are already my wife, so that's a moot point."

"Yeah, I am," I say. I step over to Lawson, grip his cheeks, and kiss him. My tongue licks along the seam of his lips and I push inside. While we are kissing, Lawson inches my dress up, bunching it at my waist, he slides his hand down my thigh and fingers my garter. "I like this," he whispers against my lips as he slips his hand between my thighs, cupping me over the satin of my panties. "You're soaked."

"Mmhmm," I moan into his mouth.

He drops to his knees and kisses me through the wet material. "Lawson," I mewl, running my fingers through his hair, pushing him into me farther. He nibbles my clit. "Please. More," I groan.

"Anything for my wife," he growls, pushing the fabric of my panties aside he thrusts two fingers inside of me and sucks my clit. "Fuuuuck!" I whisper, cupping my breasts through the silky fabric of my dress. Sliding my hand inside the sweetheart neckline, I pinch and tug my nipple, before squeezing my breast. Lawson presses his pinky to my asshole and I explode all over his face.

I'm riding out my orgasm when the door opens, "Mia—" My head snaps up to see Sydney standing there, eyes wide open. She's pushed into the room and then my eyes land on my brother. His eyes are as wide as mine when he takes in the scene before him. My hand in the top of my dress, Lawson's head between my thighs surrounded by my dress.

"Fuck, it's like your birthday all over again," Trav says, before turning on his heel and slamming the door behind him.

"I'll give you five," Syd says, before exiting the room.

"We really need to learn to lock doors," I say, as I look down Lawson. His chin glistening with my arousal.

"People need to learn to knock," he chuckles, as he stands up. "Now, bend over and let me fuck you before I marry you...again."

Turning around, I slide my panties down my legs,

lean over the small coffee table, and rest my hands on the edge of the sofa. Looking over my shoulder at Lawson, I watch as he unbuckles his pants and fumbles to get his cock out. He steps behind me and slides his cock into me.

"Lawson," I moan.

"Mia," he groans, as he thrusts himself in and out of me.

Reaching down, I press on my clit, a guttural cry breaks free. My body begins to buzz as I continue to press on my sensitive nub. Lawson's grip on my hips increases; his breathing is ragged. "Come with me, Mia."

"I'm close," I pant. He slides his hand up my side and into the top of my dress, he pinches my nipple, twisting it in that way that sets me off each and every time. My body tenses and I explode with the force of Mount Vesuvius. With his hands still inside my dress, he stills behind me and explodes, spilling his seed, groaning through his release.

I'm panting. Completely sated when there's a knock on the door. "Mia, your mom is walking down the hallway."

"Shit," I say, standing upright, the back of my head connects with Lawson's nose.

"Fuck," he groans, cupping his nose.

"Ohh, baby, I'm so sorry," I say, cupping his cheek in my palm. I try to hold back a laugh but it quickly evaporates when there's a knock at the door, and I hear Mom's voice. Grabbing Lawson's hand, I pull us into the bathroom and slam the door shut. "Shit, we're so busted."

"How is that any different for us?" he asks, as he wets a washcloth and holds it to his nose.

"True," I say with a nod. Then I realize my panties are in the other room by the sofa.

"Mia," Sydney says, knocking on the door, "Tell Lawson to put his dick away and get out of here. If your mom catches him in here, you are both dead. She'll be back in a few, I sent her on a bubbly run."

"Thanks, we'll be out in a sec."

Lawson drops the washcloth into the sink and fixes his pants and suit. My eyes rake over him. A guy in a suit is to a woman, what a chick in lingerie is to a man; fucking hot. "If you keep eye-fucking me like that, your mom is going to bust us."

"It's not my fault my husband is hot as fuck."

"Well, my wife is the sexiest woman alive."

"I knew it." We hear Sydney through the door.

Opening the door, I look at her with a confused look on my face. "I knew you two would get hitched in Vegas, your brother owes me a spa weekend."

"That dumbass should know better than to bet with you," I say with a laugh.

"What did Travis do now?" Mom says, as she steps into the room, her eyes land on Lawson and she shakes her head. "Lawson O'Connor, what are you doing here? It's bad luck to see the bride before the wedding...unless you are already married."

My mouth drops open.

Lawson's eyes widen in surprise.

And, Sydney laughs, covering her mouth to stifle the sound.

"Dammit, Mia. Now I owe your father a bottle of Johnny Walker Blue Label."

"You bet on us too?"

"Mia, your father and I have been placing bets like this our whole life."

"What else have you bet on?"

"Let's not discuss this now, and I'd appreciate it if you keep this from your father."

"Keep what from me?" Dad asks, as he steps into the room.

"Nothing," the four of us say in unison.

Dad eyes us suspiciously and then looks to me. "Mia, my God, you are stunning."

"Thanks, Daddy," I say. Stepping to him, I slide my arms around his waist and hug him. He wraps his arms around me and hugs me back.

"I totally won that bet, didn't I?" he whispers into my ear. Gently I nod my head and I can feel him quietly laugh. "Lawson, get out of here so you can marry my daughter...again."

"Dammit," Mom curses.

"It's all right, Grace," Sydney says. "You can come on the spa weekend I won from Trav."

"I knew I liked you for a reason," Mom says. She looks to Lawson. "Get out of here before you cost me anything else."

"What else have you and Dad bet on?" I question.

"Let's get you married," Mom says, changing the subject as she picks up my veil.

Taking the hint, I grab a seat on the coffee table by the sofa and discreetly pick up my panties. Sitting here with my panties in my hand, I let Mom attach the veil. Once it's in place, she steps in front of me and her eyes well with tears. "My baby girl is getting married," she cries.

"Mom, don't you start otherwise I'll start, and then I'll look like a raccoon when I get married."

Twenty minutes later, I walk down the aisle and in front of our family and friends, I say 'I do' to Lawson—wearing no panties as I didn't get a chance to slip them back on; Oops.

Epilogue

LAWSON

Leaning against the bar, I watch my wife dance with her mom and Sydney. She's beaming right now, I don't think I've ever seen her happier.

"Just remember, you hurt her and I'll kill you," Travis says from beside me.

"Are you ever going to stop with that threat?"

"Nope, she's my little sister. I don't care that you're my best friend. She's. My. Little. Sister," he enunciates those last four words while staring intently at me. A lesser man would be quivering in their boots, but I'm not just a man, I'm Lawson-fucking-O'Connor and I just married my best friend's little sister...and I'm still alive to tell the tale.

"I know, you constantly remind me of that," I say with a cocky tone, turning my gaze back to the dance floor, I watch my wife bump and grind with her mom.

"Baby sis trumps Bro Code."

"Again, I know." Turning to face him, I stare at him. "Trav, Mia and I have been together for almost two years now. She's now my wife and one day, she will be the mother to my children—"

"Ugh, I don't want to think of you and her fucking."

"You've caught us enough times to know that I get down and dirty with your baby sis," I tease.

"Fuuuuck! Don't remind me of all the times."

Mia and I have a habit of getting caught in compromising positions...and it always seems to be Trav who catches us. Then he bitches about it like the dick he's become since I hooked up with Mia.

Our moment is interrupted when Mia joins us, she slides her hand around my waist and gently squeezes my ass. "Hi, Husband."

"Hi, Wife," I say, placing my lips to her, dipping her backward. The kiss receives a round of cheers from the reception guests.

"Ugh, get a room," Travis whines.

"At least they aren't fucking," Syd says, as she sidles up to Travis.

"Give them time, it's still early."

"Challenge accepted," I say, taunting my best friend.

He flips me the bird, pulls Mia from my embrace, and drags her to the dance floor. I watch them dance and then I notice that Mia's eyes are filled with tears. A ragey stabby feeling develops in my belly, and I'm ready to murder my best friend on my wedding day, but then Mia cups her brother's face in her hands and they are laughing, and that feeling evaporates.

She walks away when Sydney cuts in. She wipes the corner of her eye as she walks over to me.

"You okay?" I say, pulling her into my arms as soon as I can reach her.

"Yeah, I think he's finally realized that we're together, and you won't ever hurt me."

"I will never hurt you, Mia. I love you with all my heart. As I said when I proposed, you are my everything. You are my forever, and today when you said I do, you made me the happiest man in the world."

"You can stop being so sweet, Lawson, you've sealed the deal." She lifts her hand to show me her engagement and wedding bands. "I'm a sure thing for the rest of your life. You are now stuck with me forever and eternity."

"And that won't be long enough, Mia."

She throws her arms over my shoulders and presses her lips to mine. I fuck her mouth with my tongue. Pulling apart, I gaze at my gorgeous wife, and realize I'm the happiest I've ever been in my life. I fell in love with my best friend's little sister and it was the best Oops I ever made.

THE END!

PLAYLIST

We Found Love – Calvin Harris feat. Rhianna

Lovefool – The Cardigans

I Wanna Dance With Somebody – Whitney Houston

Love Me Like You Do – Ellie Goulding

Firework – Katy Perry

Crazy in Love – Beyoncé

Now That We Found Love – Heavy D & the Boyz

At Last – Etta James

I Wanna Be Bad – Willa Ford

Lucky – Britney Spears

Wannabe – Spice Girls

Give My Just One Night – 98°

Why Not – Hilary Duff

I Want it That Way – The Backstreet Boys

Dirrty – Christina Aguilera

Can't Fight the Moonlight.- Leanne Rimes

Kiss Me – Sixpense Non The Richer

Complicated – Avril Lavigne
My Happy Ending – Avril Lavigne

This playlist can be found on Spotify.

ACKNOWLEDGMENTS

To my family, **Troy, Piper** and **Kade**; you three are my biggest supporters. Without you guys, I wouldn't be doing this author thing. Love you guys lots n lots.

Thank you to my editor, **Karen** from **Barren Acres Editing;** you always have my back and I'm so glad to have you on Team DL. I cannot wait for the day we meet in person.

Thank you so much to **Tash** from **Outlined with Love Designs**. I saw this cover and loved it but I dint have a story for it so I refrained. Then Oops was created and as fate would have it, it was still available. Thank you for a gorgeous cover, chapter headers for the paperback and the teasers, you really are talented and I love working with you.

Thank you **Lana Clark**, for proofreading and checking all my I's are dotted and my T's are crossed...or my he's are he's and not be's.

As usual, a shout out to my beta babes; **Andrea, Halle** and **Jenny** . Without you guys, this would be a big old mess. Thanks for your feedback, guidance and support.

And last but not least, **you, my reader**. You guys are everything to me. I love the messages, the reviews and the general banter we have. Thank you for buying and loving my books. I hope you love this story as much as I do.

Cheers,
   Dana

Read on for a sneak peek at Doc Steel, a second chance military medical romance.

PROLOGUE

...Twenty years earlier

"Are you freakin kidding me, Griff?" she shouts, her voice laced with anger, shock, and sadness. "You accept this without talking to me first?" This is not how I expected her to react. I expected excitement and happiness. Not like this.

The 'this' Autumn is referring to is I just joined the navy and entered into their medical training program. I was amazed at what they offered in regard to the training and immediately signed up. Sure, I was shocked I enlisted, it was never on my radar, but it was too good of an offer to pass up. Not only will my degree be covered by the government but they will also pay me to study. I was so excited; I accepted immediately and couldn't wait to tell Autumn the news. This will be a huge financial relief for us; the only downfall is I need to move to Portsmouth, Virginia. I was sure Autumn would be happy and excited for me. For us. I certainly didn't think she'd react like this.

"I thought I was doing the right thing," I plead, "My degree will be paid for, sure I have to serve, but in the long run, it will be great for us."

"No, Griff, it will be great for you. While you are off sailing the high seas, I'll be here. Alone." She wipes her eyes, which are now glassy with tears. "I can't believe you are going to walk away from us."

"I'm not walking away from us. I'm doing this for us. Don't you see?"

She stares at me, the first tear falls and she angrily wipes it away. "No, this is all for you."

With those words, she turns and walks away from me. Racing over to her, I grab her hand and spin her to face me. We stare at one another. Her eyes well with tears and she begins to sob uncontrollably. Lifting my hand, I wipe away her tears. Bending down, I rest my forehead against her. "Autumn, I promise this will all work out. I need you to trust me."

"I do trust you, but I just don't see how you being a million miles away will work." She swallows back a sob, "Please don't do this."

"I'm sorry, I have to."

She sighs deeply, I can finally see acceptance whirring around in her face. "When do you leave?"

My lips lift in a smile, I knew she'd come around. "In two weeks."

"What?" she screeches. "I thought we'd have more time."

"I know, me too, but now you see why I had to make this decision as quickly as I did."

She nods. "I understand," she mumbles but really she doesn't, she just said that to appease me.

"I love you, Autumn," I vow, placing a kiss on her forehead.

"I love you too, forever and eternity," she whispers back to me.

Forever and eternity, that's what we always said to one another, and I really hope that our love mantra is true.

The next two weeks, all we do is fight and bicker about anything and everything. I try everything to get her to see this is great for us. I even try to get her to come with me. She doesn't want to leave Sandpoint, it is her home. Her family and friends are here. I want her to be happy, so I stopped asking her to move with me. After a long discussion, we agree to stay together but I know we won't, there is too much hurt in her heart.

The morning I leave, she is cold and distant. I know I've already lost her. On one hand I am excited for the venture ahead, but on the other, I am losing the one I love unconditionally. We kiss goodbye but there is no passion in it, it is robotic. She stands there and watches as I walk toward the plane. The plane taking me to Portsmouth, Virginia, where I will one day become Doctor Griffin Steel.

At the top of the stairs, I look back at her and my heart broke. She is crouched down, staring at the plane, tears streaming down her face. And I know: those tears and her heartbreak are because of me. In that moment, I start to wonder if maybe I'm making a mistake...career-wise, it is the best decision I ever made. In regard to Autumn; it is a huge mistake.

Doc Steel is now available to buy or read as part of your Kindle Unlimited subscription.

The Unexpected Gift

The Unexpected Letter

The Unexpected Package

The Unexpected Connection

THE CASTAWAY GROVE COLLECTION

Love has arrived in the Grove

Oasis

Unequivocal Love

Five Words

Broken Rules

...and a few more as well.

THE LIQUOR CABINET SERIES

Liquor has never been so disturbingly saucy

Malt Me (Book 1)

Tequila Healing (Book 2)

Wine Not (Book 3)

The Final Shot (Book 4)

The Liquor Cabinet: Series boxset

FACEBOOK ~ INSTAGRAM ~ BOOKBUB

GOODREADS ~ WEBSITE

dlgallieauthor@outlook.com

Sign up to my newsletter

ABOUT THE AUTHOR

DL Gallie is from Queensland, Australia, but she's lived in many different places all over the world, including the UK and Canada. She currently resides in Central Queensland with her husband and two munchkins. She and her husband have been together since she was sixteen, and although they—code for me—drive each other crazy at times, she couldn't imagine her life without him.

Shortly after her son was born, DL began heavily reading again. With encouragement from her husband, she picked up the pen and started writing, and now the voices in her head won't shut up.

DL enjoys listening to music, drinking white wine in the summer, red wine in the winter, and beer all year round. She's also never been known to turn down a cocktail, especially a margarita.